Christmas COUNTRY Classics

Stories: Caleb Pirtle III   Illustrations: Brenda Keene

Published by Heritage Publishing, Inc., 1720 Regal Row, Suite 228, Dallas, Texas 75235.
(214) 630-4300 (800) 520-2665

Publisher	Rodney L. Dockery
Editorial Director	Caleb Pirtle III
Executive Editor	Kenneth E. Lively
Production Editor	Marnie Burkett
Staff Writer	Bob Perkins, Jr.
Editorial Assistant	Leigh Ann Linney
Art Director	Janet Bergin Todd
Illustrator	Brenda Keene
Vice President / Corporate Sales	Darrell Pesek

First Printing

Printed through Bidal Group: David Terrazas, President.

Manufactured in the United States of America

Contents

'Twas The Night
Before A Country Christmas

'Twas the night before Christmas
    And down the long road
The chilled winds were blowing
    In the woods where it snowed.

A mist hung like a blanket
    So gray in the trees,
Fog crept in on cat's feet
    And sat on the leaves.

The bunnies had snuggled
    Down where it was warm,
Deep in their den
    On the Butterworth farm.

The chickens quit scratching
    For feed in the dirt,
The frost on their feathers
    So cold that it hurt.

The cattle had heard
    The old dog when he barked;
They were trying to get back
    To the barn before dark.

The woodchuck crawled out
    Of his hole in the ground
And faraway saw
    The dim lights of the town,

Where children were dreaming
    Of tiny reindeer
In hopes that Saint Nick
    Would remember this year

That they all lived back
    Where the winding roads crossed,
Beyond the tall mountains
    Where grown men got lost.

Their stockings were hanging
    Just over the door
In cabins Saint Nick
    Never visited before.

The girls wanted new dolls,
    The boys baseball caps,
But their town, alas,
    Was not marked on the map.

From out of the night
    There arose such a clatter
The animals woke up
    To see what was the matter.

Something had fallen
From out of the sky
And crashed in the north woods
While trying to fly.

The dog left his fast tracks
Cut deep in the snow
And everyone followed;
They knew where to go.

And what they beheld
Was a curious sight,
A round little man
With a curious plight.

The jolly old gent,
With his head hanging low,
Was spittin' and sputterin',
His beard full of snow.

He sat for a moment
And looked all around
That jolly old laughter
Replaced by a frown.

The red rooster shouted
      While chilled winds did blow,
"What happened to you, sir?"
      He wanted to know.

Saint Nick brushed his red suit
      Which melted the frost.
"I hate to admit it," he said,
      "But I'm lost.

"I took a wrong turn 'cause
      The light sure was dim;
The next thing I knew
      I had hit a tree limb."

His reindeer were breathless
      Their lines all entangled;
The bell on his sleigh
      Was too broken to jangle.

His shoulders were sagging,
      A tear left his eye,
The bunnies felt bad
      For the saddened old guy.

"The world's full of children
    Just waiting for me,"
He said, "And I'm stuck
    Way out here in the trees.

"The children will think
    That I no longer care
If Christmas morn, comes
    And I haven't been there."

"Don't worry, Saint Nick,"
    Said the wizened old dog,
"It won't take us long
    To get out of this fog.

"I'll lead you down backroads
    For miles all around.
And the woodchuck knows places
    I've not even found.

"In case you got hungry
    While facing those winds,
Here's milk from the cow,
    And an egg from the hen.

"Before you start flying
    Away from this farm,
Hold on to the bunny;
    He'll keep your hands warm."

Saint Nick wore a new grin
    At least a mile wide,
And so did the reindeer
    Grouped up at his side.

He had worried that Christmas
    Would not come this year
If he couldn't find a quick way
    out of here.

Now he could face
    The long, cold night ahead,
"Just how can I thank you?"
    Was all that he said.

"We've got all that we need"
    Said the dog, laying down,
"But stay long enough
    For the children in town.

"They've all heard about you
    And your eight reindeer
But the stockings they hang
    Remain empty each year."

None of the children
       Wanted to be missed.
Santa looked through his coat.
       There wasn't a list.

He had no idea
       Who was naughty or good,
He'd bring what they wanted
       If only he could.

The old dog smiled broadly
       And took Saint Nick's arm.
"Don't worry," he said,
       "There's no cause for alarm.

"This is my neighborhood.
       These are my friends.
I know where they live
       And what makes them all grin."

The old dog waved proudly
       Toward his neighborhood
Saying, "Don't worry, Santa,
       My friends are all good."

Dasher moved through the forest,
       With Dancer behind,
As Prancer and Vixen
       Strained hard at the lines.

Comet ran with the North Wind,
Cupid just couldn't stop.
Donner and Blitzen
Headed for the rooftops.

Saint Nick's down the chimneys,
His bag full of toys,
Too quiet and too careful
To make any noise.

Christmas at daybreak is
Covered with frost,
Down in the town
Where the winding roads cross.

The children are laughing,
And Santa can't fret,
For this is one Christmas
He didn't forget.

Their stockings are filled,
And their spirits are high.
But only the critters
And woodlands know why.

The Christmas Haunting Of Ebb Scrooge

The chilled December morning
had turned to flannel gray
as Ebb Scrooge walked into the lobby
of his Caprock bank,
frost on his breath,
and his hands were numb.
He was a tight-fisted rancher
and a frugal banker,
always looking for a deal
where he could talk some farmer
out of his last dollar
if necessary.
His face was as gray as his hair,
worn with wrinkles,
and he leaned heavily on his cane.
He had no friends,
and wanted none,
and he glanced into the office
where his partner, Jake Marley,
had worked for so many years.

But Jake was gone.
He had simply up and died
at least six years ago,
which had not been a friendly
thing to do,
leaving Ebb Scrooge to run
the bank alone.
Scrooge laughed to himself,
and his laugh was as cold,
as frosty,
as the biting wind outside.
Sure he missed old Jake,
but now he didn't have to split
his profits with anybody,
which made Christmas about as merry
as it could get.

Scrooge heard the sounds
of Christmas echo
down the streets outside his bank,
and it was a gloomy sound.
At least it was to him.
Christmas simply meant people
were taking their money out of his bank
and using it to buy gifts,
and he hated for anybody
to take their money away from him.
He believed it was his
even when it wasn't.

Jake Marley

Somebody had foolishly put up
a Christmas tree in the lobby
of the bank,
but Scrooge dragged it into the alley
out back
and threw it away.
Bah. Humbug.
He preferred the cold, wet rain
to Christmas.

Scrooge heard a knock
and saw Bob Cratchit walk
through the door
of his office
with snow dripping off his coat.
Cratchit was his ranch foreman,
a good man with cattle,
a good man fixing fence,
a good man plowing new ground,
but Scrooge would have never hired him
if Cratchit had not been his
oldest sister's youngest son.

"Merry Christmas, Uncle Scrooge,"
Cratchit said, and Scrooge frowned,
when he heard his foreman say,
"We'd like for you to join us
this Christmas day.
We've got a roasted turkey
and a pot of bread pudding,
and Tiny Tim himself has set
a special plate for you."
Bah. Humbug.
Scrooge was saying,
"The fence is broke
down in the north pasture.
I want another corral built
back behind the stables.
And the barn roof has a leak.
I'll be at work on Christmas Day,
and I expect you to do the same.
Christmas is just another day
to me, a time to fix what's broke
and keep it fixed."

Old Ebb's eyes were as chilly
as a dark, winter's day.
All Bob Cratchit could do was
softly mutter, "Merry Christmas," as
he backed out of the office,
leaving Scrooge alone,
which is the way he liked to be.

The clock struck six.
It was already dark.
Scrooge gathered his workers
in the lobby and told them,
"The bank won't open tomorrow
at nine, as usual.
It'll open at ten,
and I expect you to be here.

The bank may be closed to
customers, but it won't be
closed to employees, provided,
of course,
they want to remain employees
of the Caprock National Bank."
Scrooge left them all with sad
and disappointed faces,
and he hurried out of town so
he would no longer have to hear
those awful sounds of Christmas.
The cold, north winds wiped
the snowflakes off the dirt road
that led up to the gables
of his dark and dreary home.

12

Scrooge stumbled
through the dim hallway
of a cold and cheerless house
that was a lot like him.
He glanced in the mirror,
and behind his own image
was an eerie, ghostly face
with eerie, ghostly eyes
and it looked a lot
like old Jake Marley's face.
His knees began to weaken.

His spine tingled.
And the eerie, ghostly face
with eerie, ghostly eyes faded.
And all he saw in the mirror
was his own wrinkled face.
Old Scrooge went to bed
without supper,
wondering why
a wealthy man like himself
saw ghosties in the dark.

A bell rang softly in the dark,
and a chain rattled,
and grandfather's clock was ticking
just a little too loud,
and grandfather's clock
had not ticked in years.
Scrooge heard footsteps
coming, creeping, down the hall.
The oak door opened
and a strange sight appeared
wearing Marley's coat
with Marley's hat upon his head
and Marley's boots upon his feet.

"For six long years
I've walked the land, a captive
of these chains," Jake Marley said,
his eyes like burning coals.
"There was a time when all
I cared about was money, but
money can't help me now.
I am doomed to wander lost
until the end of time.
But you can escape my fate,
my friend.
There is still time for you.

14

Tonight will be the longest night
that you will ever spend.
You are at the mercy of three ghosts,
and the first will come
before the clock strikes one.
Listen and learn,
my friend," he said,
"to help someone in need.
Or you, too, will be doomed
to drift from place to place,
weighed down by these terrible chains."

The chime of one awakened Scrooge,
and a bony hand
belonging to the bony spirit
of a bony man
touched his hot and fearful face.
The spirit's laughter was a cackle,
and he whispered, "Come with me,
for you must see
the ghosts of Christmas Past."

And off they went to a far away
Christmas night,
so long ago,
when the lights burned bright,
and the dancers danced,
and singers sang
inside Amos Springer's barn.

Laughter spun like music
atop the rafters in the barn,
but Amy Sue, so all alone,
had teardrops on her face.
Ebb saw himself beside her,
and he thought his eyes had lied,
for he looked so very young,
and she looked so very sad.

"I cannot marry you," she said
to the brash young man
named Ebeneezer Scrooge,

"for you love your money
more than me,
even more than life itself."
And she turned away,
and he turned away,
and Scrooge felt a sharp pain
in his heart,
the same pain he had felt
the night he lost the only girl
he ever asked to be his wife.
His was a hard heart, they said.
And no one ever knew that,
once upon a time, it had been broken.
"All that's important," whispered
the ghost,
"is that you know what you've gained
in life and what you've lost."
In an instant Scrooge was home,
and his heart still ached,
and he was alone, always alone,
as bitter as before.

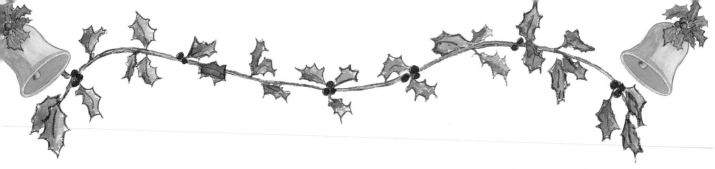

Three times the old clock chimed,
and from the shadows there came
a giant of a man
with a booming voice and laughter
that filled the cold room with warmth.
Holly was wrapped around the crown
and icicles hung from the brim
of his hat.
The ghost of Christmas Present
beckoned Scrooge and took
the old man's hand,

and they walked together
through the snow
down the winding dirt road
to poor Bob Cratchit's house.
Through the window Ebb could see
fire crackling in the chimney
and a Christmas tree with lights
that glistened like the stars
beyond the snow clouds.
Beneath the tree were toys and games
and a tiny gift from Tiny Tim
that had old Scrooge's name.

Bob Cratchit stumbled
through the door with Tim
perched upon his shoulders.
They laughed, so happy, all of them,
but the boy looked so pale and thin.
He carried a little crutch
his father had whittled
from a hickory tree, for
his legs were withered away.
Yet his smile lit up the room,
and he hugged his father
and his mother,
and he sang out loud
for all the world,
"God, bless us everyone."

The ghost of Christmas Present
glanced away, a tear hanging in his eye.
"Next year, the boy's chair is empty,"
he said, "and the crutch lies useless
on the floor.
Dark shadows hover over this house,
and if they remain unchanged,
Tiny Tim will never celebrate
another Christmas.
This will be his last."

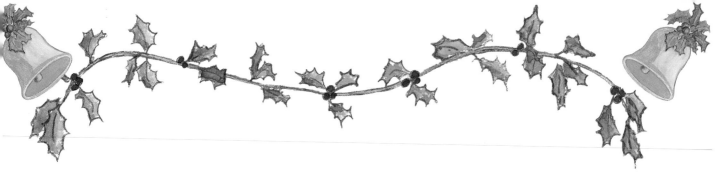

The old man looked back inside
at the gentle smile on Tiny Tim's face.
He was just a wee lad
with crippled legs,
barely able to drag himself
across the floor
with his little homemade crutch.
But there was joy in his smile.
The world would be so cold,
so empty,
without Tiny Tim's smile.

Scrooge turned again
and found himself trapped
in the dark, deep woods,
the night a little blacker,
the wind a little colder
than it had ever been before.

The ghost was gone.
The cabin had faded into a mist.
And Tiny Tim's smile
had faded away with it.

A hooded figure
walked through the forest
toward Scrooge.
He had no face, no eyes,
and Ebb's stomach tightened into knots.
The first spirit had startled him.
The second ghost had surprised him.
The one with no face and no eyes
frightened him.

He had not been scared this badly
since he thought he lost his bank book.
The ghost of Christmas Yet To Come
motioned silently for Scrooge
to follow,
and the old man followed,
afraid to go, afraid not to.

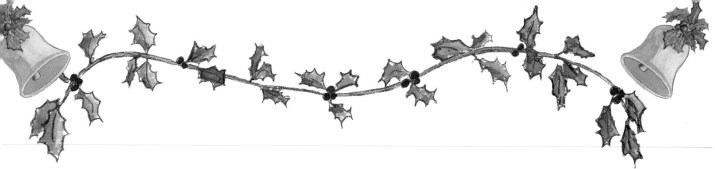

Before them appeared
the cabin of Bob Cratchit,
a home no longer filled with laughter.
Sadness dwelled
where happiness had lived.
Tiny Tim was nowhere around.
Tiny Tim's chair was empty.
A crutch lay useless
beside the bed.

"What will Christmas be like
without our Tiny Tim?"
the boy's mother asked
with a tear stain in her voice.

Bob Cratchit tried to smile,
and he said, "We shall remember
that his kindness, patience,
laughter and love were
the greatest gifts anyone
ever received. And we shall
go through life, trying to give
those gifts to others."
And like Tiny Tim,
before Ebb's eyes,
the cabin disappeared.

Scrooge ran hard
through the woodland,
passing an iron gate
that opened into
an old-fashioned churchyard,
choked with bristle grass
and frost-covered weeds.
No one came there anymore.
No one had a reason to come
there anymore.

Ebb fell beside a grave,
his heart pounding,
and his mouth was dry.
Never had a night been
so dreary and cold.
Never had a grave looked
so lonely and forlorn.
And upon a gray, granite
piece of rock, Scrooge saw
his own name scratched
into the stone.

The grave was his own,
and he fell face down
upon the bristle grass.
It was not the thought
of dying that troubled him.
It was the fact
that no one cared.

22

He had died and been forgotten.
And he knew
down deep in his heart
that Tiny Tim would not
have forgotten him.
He rose to his knees
and looked at the ghost who wore the
hooded cape
where there was no face
and no eyes, and he said,
"I don't have to be the man
I was. I can change.

I'll make sure the spirit
of Christmas lives every day.
I can't change the past.
It's already gone.
But I can make a difference
in today and tomorrow."
He reached out to grasp
the bony hand,
but the bony hand became
the icy bedpost of his bed.

The early morning sun
found old Ebb Scrooge
driving down the snowy
streets of Caprock,
and all around him the
silver Christmas bells
were ringing.
The music sounded so familiar
that Scrooge sang along,

and it surprised him because
he did not know the songs.

He was standing at the bank
when the clock struck ten,
and he gave each employee
a Christmas bonus
then sent them all back home again.

He asked the plump little lady
with the Salvation Army Bell
just how many dollars she thought
her kettle would hold.
"Two hundred," she answered.
He gave her a check for five hundred.
"Consider it full," he said,
"and go on home to your family.
And if there's a child in Caprock

who doesn't have a gift to open this
year,
just let me know."

"God bless you," was all she said,
and Ebb told her,
"God bless us everyone,"
remembering the smile
on Tiny Tim's face
when he said it first of all.

Scrooge found Bob Cratchit
lying in the snow,
working hard on a fence
where he had been
since the first light
of Christmas touched the fields.
"This is no place to be today,"
the old man said. "What you've
got to do has waited this long,
and it will wait another day.
Besides, you promised me
a Christmas dinner."
Bob Cratchit grinned and said, "We
always have an extra plate for you."

26

As they drove back through
a mist of snow, Ebb Scrooge said,
"I called a city doctor, one who
fixes broken, withered limbs,
and he can straighten out
the crooked legs
that have crippled Tiny Tim.
You take good care of the boy,"
he said, "and I'll take care
of the cost."
It was the first time
Bob Cratchit had shed a tear
in years,
the first time he had ever
cried and laughed
at the same time.

Ebb Scrooge walked into the cabin,
loaded down with gifts,
and Tiny Tim crawled into his lap.
The toys were wonderful,
the boy said,
the best he ever had.
But what he liked best,
and what he always liked best,
was having Uncle Scrooge
drop by for Christmas dinner.

27

Ebb stared across the table
at the chair where the boy
always sat.
It would not be empty
this Christmas,
nor next Christmas,
not until the boy was grown
and had a family of his own.
In his heart dwelt the spirit
of Christmas.
It was all the boy had to give.
It was the best gift of them all.

Rudolph The Red Nosed Reindeer Finds His Glow Again

Rudolph the red nosed reindeer
crept down to the river's edge
at daybreak
and stared with disbelief
into the cold water
that looked more like a mirror
in the morning sun.

The critters hiding in the forest
could not believe their eyes,
and Rudolph felt his knees
begin to quiver.
He did not even recognize
his own reflection.
The glow had vanished
from his nose.

He was nothing
without his red nose.
He was just a common reindeer
if he lost his wonderful glow,
and Santa Claus would no longer
need him to light the way
and guide him
through the darkness
of Christmas Eve.

Rudolph ran into the hollow
of the tall and stately pines,
wondering why
his beautiful red nose
had turned to brown,
an ugly brown, and,
as teardrops tumbled
from his eyelids,
he wished he had never been born.

Then the robins came to tell him
that the beaver dam had broken,
and the rushing water
was rushing toward
the briar root home
of the little elfin family
down where the blackberries grew.

Rudolph quickly dried
his tears.
There was no time for pity
or feeling sorry for himself.
He raced toward the lake of plenty,
running wild and free,
searching for the lost elf family
and the little elfin child
that played hide-and-seek
in the forest.

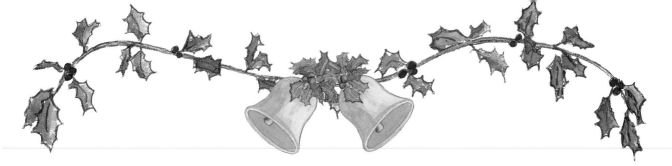

He saw them clinging
to a ragged oak leaf,
as a raging whirlpool spun them
round and round,
and Rudolph jumped,
without thinking,
into the river.
Churning water
almost drowned him.
A pebble poked him in the eye.

The elves all hung together,
hand in hand,
fighting the rapids that tried
to tear them apart.
The currents pushed Rudolph
farther down the stream,
and he battled the angry water,
past snow
and ice,
cold and numb,
aware only that the elfin family
needed him,
and he could never, never quit.

Tiny little hooves touched bottom
down amidst the rocks and mud.
Fear gripped Rudolph.
He could no longer see
the elfin family,
and they were all at the mercy
of the wild and raging flood.
He called for the elfin child.
He called for his littlest friend.
But all he heard were the sounds
of rushing water
and his own ragged breath.

Rudolph regained the surface,
tearing through the old oak roots,
past the leaves
and fallen branches,
reaching for the elf child's hand,
holding him tightly
while the little elfin family
climbed upon his weary back
and rode toward dry land.

There was shelter in the hollow,
a refuge from the falling snow.
They sprawled exhausted
on the ground,
soaked and cold,
but still alive,
and the elf child was asleep
by sundown,
his little hand resting gently
on the tip of Rudolph's nose.

And when the morning sun awoke
them,
Rudolph was just as startled
as he had been before.
Reflections in the water
never lied to him,
and reflections in the water
showed him that,
once again,
his nose had a glow so red
and so bright
he could not wait for Christmas night.

He loved the little elf child,
for the elfin
was his friend.
And the love he felt,
and the love he gave,
had made his nose shine again.

On Christmas Eve
you can see them,
no matter how foggy,
no matter how dark,
just ahead of Santa's pack.
There's Rudolph out front
where he's supposed to be
with the elfin
just a shadow on his back.

Frosty The Snowman Never Leaves Forever

Frosty the snowman
stood beneath the morning sun,
and he could no longer feel
a chill in the air.
The clouds had left with the night,
and the snow had gone with them,
and his hands were melting
beneath his hand-me-down mittens.

His old top hat didn't fit quite
so snug anymore, and his smile had
grown crooked even though Frosty was
as happy-go-lucky as he had ever been.
Yet winter was leaving him, and in the
distance he heard the spring birds singing,
and a little patch of snow began sliding slowly
from the rooftop on the barn.

Frosty had not looked forward to this day,
but he knew it was coming anyway,
and his old top hat began to slip down
around the two pieces of coal that had been
his eyes since the first November snowfall.

He heard the children running before he saw them,
hurrying down the wooded, country lane,
trying to reach their friend before the spring sun
warmed up and took him away again.

They plucked his top hat from his head
and gently removed a ragged old coat
that Frosty had worn since the smallest
child of all had spent his last quarter
to buy it from a churchyard
Christmas sale.

The children placed their little arms
around him and held on tight
so he could not
go away, pleading for Frosty
to stay with them forever.

Frosty wiped away their little tears
as a puddle formed from the
melting snow
beneath him. Don't be sad, he said.
It's just time for me to go and
chase the winter
down before it leaves me too far behind.
But I'll be back next year.
Just wait and see.
I'll ride back on the cold north wind
and you can find me down the lane
beside the lake when the snow
begins to fall again.
I'll just be a bunch of flakes then.
But we all have to start from somewhere.
And if I can start from anywhere
in the world,
I want to start with all of you.

The Gift
Of The Drummer Boy's Song

The little drummer boy
was always alone.
But
he was never lonely.

He lived in a world
of his own,
a special place,
and the animals would trail
along after him
through the country forests
of the northern woodlands.

His clothes were
in patches,
and his shoes
both had holes,
but the smile
on his face
was his fortune.

The little drummer boy
sometimes thought
he heard the wind
whispering his name.
He never answered,
but
it always made him smile.

And he marched
through the woodlands,
drumming the sun up
and
drumming the sun down
and
hearing the most beautiful music
in the world
in his drum.
He was always out of step
with everyone else.
And
he was always in a hurry,
even when he had
no place to go.

He wasn't really different,
no matter
what the others said.
He wasn't really different.
The little drummer boy
didn't think he was.

At night he looked
into a velvet sky
and saw
the first star of Christmas,
and he would whisper,
"It's mine,
all mine."

The animals never laughed
at the little drummer boy,
no matter what he thought,
no matter what he did.
He came to the barn
and gave them hay
and oats
and a song on his drum.

They didn't care
if he might be different.
He loved them,
and they loved him,
and after all,
the first star of Christmas
must belong
to somebody.

He drummed
for his friends,
and he drummed
for himself,
and he drummed
for the star
in the sky.

On Christmas Eve,
lights by the millions
draped the small town,

as one
by one
they came
from every neighborhood
to decorate
the tree in the square.

Stars
and
angels,
candy canes
and
brightly colored balls
were placed
upon each limb.

But the drummer boy
watched from afar,
alone
and never alone,
waiting with the animals
to see each boy
and girl
leave a gift
upon the tree
in honor of the Christ child.

He reached
into his pocket,
and it was empty.
All he owned
was a smile
and a drum
and the first star of Christmas.

He winked
at the star
and smiled his best smile,
and when everyone was gone,
and the street was bare,
he tied his drum
on the bottom limb
and prayed that the Christ child
loved it
as much as he.

He had so little.
He gave so much.
And
all night long
the wind
and the branches
softly played
the beat
of the drummer boy's song.

It drummed the sun up
and
it drummed the sun down
and
he knew
that somewhere above,
the Christ child was
listening;
the Christ child had heard
the gift
of a song on the drum.

44